The Girl Who Cried Flowers

and Other Tales

The Girl Who Cried Flowers

and Other Tales

BY JANE YOLEN

Illustrated by David Palladini

Schocken Books • New York

ALSO BY JANE YOLEN

The Bird of Time
The Boy Who Had Wings
The Girl Who Loved the Wind
The Wizard Islands

First published by Schocken Books 1981
10 9 8 7 6 5 4 3 2 1   81 82 83 84

Text copyright © 1974 by Jane Yolen
Illustrations copyright © 1974 by David Palladini

Designed by Sallie Baldwin

Manufactured in the United States of America
ISBN 0–8052–0666–3

Library of Congress Cataloging in Publication Data is on page 56

Contents

For David:
Yesterday,
Today, Tomorrow

In ancient Greece, where the spirits of beautiful women were said to dwell in trees, a girl was born who cried flowers. Tears never fell from her eyes. Instead blossoms cascaded down her cheeks: scarlet, gold, and blue in the spring, and snow-white in the fall.

No one knew her real mother and father. She had been found one day wrapped in a blanket of woven grasses in the crook of an olive tree. The shepherd who found her called her Olivia after the tree and brought her home to his childless wife. Olivia lived with them as their daughter, and grew into a beautiful girl.

At first her strangeness frightened the villagers. But after a while, Olivia charmed them all with her gentle, giving nature. It was not long before the villagers were showing her off to any traveler who passed their way. For every stranger, Olivia would squeeze a tiny tear-blossom from her eyes. And that is how her fame spread throughout the land.

But soon a tiny tear-blossom was not enough. Young men wanted nosegays to give to the girls they courted. Young women wanted garlands to twine in their hair. The priests asked for bouquets to bank their altars. And old men and women begged funeral wreaths against the time of their deaths.

To all these requests, Olivia said yes. And so she had to spend her days thinking sad thoughts, listening to tragic tales, and crying mountains of flowers to make other people happy. Still, she did not complain, for above all things Olivia loved making other people happy—even though it made her sad.

Then one day, when she was out in her garden looking at the far mountains and trying to think of sad things to fill her mind, a young man came by. He was strong enough for two, but wise enough to ask for help when he needed it. He had heard of Olivia's magical tears and had come to beg a garland for his own proud sweetheart.

But when he saw Olivia, the thought of his proud sweetheart went entirely out of the young man's mind. He sat down by Olivia's feet and started to tell her tales, for though he was a farmer, he had the gift of telling that only true storytellers have. Soon Olivia was smiling, then laughing in delight, as the tales rolled off his tongue.

"Stop," she said at last. "I do not even know your name."

"I am called Panos," he said.

"Then, Panos, if you must tell me tales—and indeed I hope you never stop—tell me sad ones. I must fill myself with sorrow if I am to give you what you want."

"I want only you," he said, for his errand had been long forgotten. "And that is a joyous thing."

For a time it was true. Panos and Olivia were married and

lived happily in a small house at the end of the village. Panos worked long hours in the fields while Olivia kept their home neat and spotless. In the evenings they laughed together over Panos' stories or over the happenings of the day, for Panos had forbidden Olivia ever to cry again. He said it made him sad to see her sad. And as she wanted only to make him happy, Olivia never let even the smallest tear come to her eyes.

But one day, an old lady waited until Panos had gone off to the fields and then came to Olivia's house to borrow a cup of oil.

"How goes it?" asked Olivia innocently, for since her marriage to Panos, she had all but forsaken the villagers. And indeed, since she would not cry flowers for them, the villagers had forsaken her in return.

The old lady sighed. She was fine, she explained, but for one small thing. Her granddaughter was being married in the morning and needed a crown of blue and gold flowers. But, the crafty old lady said, since Olivia was forbidden to cry any more blossoms her granddaughter would have to go to the wedding with none.

"If only I could make her just one small crown," thought Olivia. She became so sad at the thought that she could not give the girl flowers without hurting Panos that tears came unbidden to her eyes. They welled up, and as they started down her cheeks, they turned to petals and fluttered to the floor.

The old lady quickly gathered up the blossoms and, without a word more, left for home.

Soon all the old ladies were stopping by for a cup of oil. The old men, too, found excuses to stray by Olivia's door. Even the priest paid her a call and, after telling Olivia all the troubles of the parish, left with a bouquet for the altar of his church.

All this time Panos was unaware of what was happening. But he saw that Olivia was growing thin, that her cheeks were furrowed, and her eyes rimmed with dark circles. He realized that she barely slept at night. And so he tried to question her.

"What is it, dear heart?" he asked out of love.

But Olivia did not dare answer.

"Who has been here?" he roared out of fear.

But Olivia was still. Whatever she answered would have been wrong. So she turned her head and held back the tears just as Panos wished, letting them go only during the day when they would be useful to strangers.

One day, when Olivia was weeping a basket full of Maiden's Breath for a wedding, Panos came home unexpectedly from the fields. He stood in the doorway and stared at Olivia who sat on the floor surrounded by the lacy blossoms.

Panos knew then all that had happened. What he did not know was why. He held up his hands as if in prayer, but his face was filled with anger. He could not say a word.

Olivia looked at him, blossoms streaming from her eyes. "How can I give you what you want?" she asked. "How can I give *all* of you what you want?"

Panos had no answer for her but the anger in his face. Olivia jumped up and ran past him out the door.

All that day Panos stayed in the house. His anger was so fierce he could not move. But by the time evening came, his anger had turned to sadness, and he went out to look for his wife.

Though the sun had set, he searched for her, following the trail of flowers. All that night the scent of the blossoms led him around the village and through the olive groves. Just as the sun was rising, the flowers ended at the tree where Olivia had first been found.

Under the tree was a small house made entirely of flowers, just large enough for a single person. Its roof was of scarlet lilies and its walls of green ivy. The door was blue Glory-of-the-snow and the handle a blood-red rose.

Panos called out, "Olivia?" but there was no answer. He put his hand to the rose handle and pushed the door open. As he opened the door, the rose thorns pierced his palm, and a single drop of his blood fell to the ground.

Panos looked inside the house of flowers, but Olivia was not there. Then he felt something move at his feet, and he looked down.

Where his blood had touched the ground, a small olive tree was beginning to grow. As Panos watched, the tree grew until it pushed up the roof of the house. Its leaves became crowned with the scarlet lilies. And as Panos looked closely at the twisted trunk of the tree, he saw the figure of a woman.

"Olivia," he cried, for indeed it was she.

Panos built a small hut by the tree and lived there for the rest of his life. The olive tree was a strange one, unlike any of the others in the grove. For among its branches twined every kind of flower. Its leaves were covered with the softest petals: scarlet, gold, and blue in the spring, and snow-white in the fall. There were always enough flowers on the tree for anyone who asked, as well as olives enough for Panos to eat and to sell.

It was said by the villagers—who guessed what they did not know—that each night a beautiful woman came out of the tree and stayed with Panos in his hut until dawn.

When at last Panos grew old and died, he was buried under the tree. Though the tree grew for many years more, it never had another blossom. And all the olives that it bore from then on were as bitter and salty as tears.

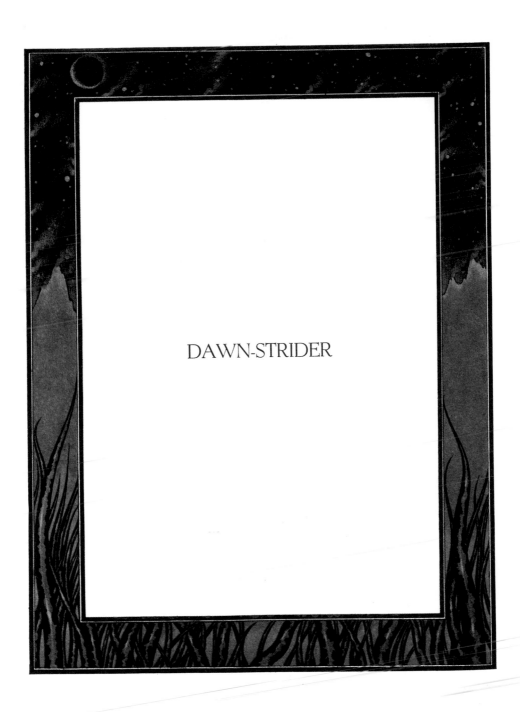

DAWN-STRIDER

Far, far to the East, before the sun had settled firmly on a route, there lived a giant who walked at night.

His black head seemed crowned with the stars. The earth thundered where he stepped. And all who saw or heard him were afraid.

Night after lonely night the giant made his rounds. Up the mountains and down. By hill towns and valleys. Through low places and high. His footsteps warned of his coming, and the ways were empty where he walked.

Some people said that it was his nature to walk at night. Others, older, who remembered beginnings even as they forgot endings, recalled how the giant had once walked by day. But one morning, by chance, he had seen his own reflection in a still mountain lake. He had been so dismayed by his own rough image that he had taken to the night and had walked in darkness ever since.

One night, lost in a waking dream, the giant missed the crowing of the cock that warned of the coming sun. Instead of going straightaway to his castle, which was hollowed in a cave, he stopped by the side of a stream to drink.

As he knelt, he heard a whisper of grass. Then he heard a soughing of wind. At last he heard the sound of early morning flowers opening.

Turning quickly, the giant saw a child dressed in red and gold.

"Who are you?" he asked.

Before the child could answer, the giant growled: "Don't you know that I am Night-Walker? All who hear and see me are afraid." He stood up against the sky and his shadow put out the lingering stars.

The child answered, "And why should I be afraid?"

"They say my face withers the eyes. They say the sound of my coming turns hearers to stone."

"I have seen and I have heard," said the child. "But I am here still."

"Who are you?" the giant asked again.

"I am Dawn-Strider. And where I come, the sun comes, too."

"The sun!" cried the giant, and he looked about fearfully.

"And are you afraid of me?" asked the child with a laugh.

But the giant did not hear. He had already started to run, leaving hollows in the ground where he stepped.

For two nights the giant cowered in his cave and thought about the child who was not afraid. But on the third night, a night of dark shadows, he ventured out. He was determined to capture Dawn-Strider. For, in his own way, the giant had fallen in love with the child, the only being who did not hide at his coming. He wanted to carry Dawn-Strider to his cave-castle home.

Slowly the giant walked to the stream where he had seen the child and knelt down by the bank. First with his hand he scooped out a large deep basin in the earth near the side of the stream. He lined it with the softest mosses and made a break-fall of pine and fern. Finally, he covered the hole with juniper and trailed wild grapevines over the boughs.

Then Night-Walker lay down beside the trap to wait for the dawn.

When he heard the grass whisper and the wind sough through the juniper, and when he heard the sounds of flowers opening, the giant knew that Dawn-Strider would soon be there. So he began to moan.

Before long, Dawn-Strider appeared by the stream. "Why do you lie so still? Why do you cry?" the child asked.

The giant made no answer but continued to moan.

Dawn-Strider came over to his side and knelt down to see what was wrong. But as he came close to the giant, the child broke through the grapevines and juniper and fell into the hole.

Immediately the giant leaped up and looked into the trap. Then, smiling for the first time, he reached down and picked the child up in one hand. With great thundering steps, he ran back to his castle in the cave. Once they were inside, he rolled a huge stone over the entrance.

"Why did you trick me? Why did you carry me off to

this dark castle?" asked the child when they were seated in the cave.

"Because I want you to stay with me always," replied the giant.

"But if you had asked," said the child, "I would have come by myself."

"Oh, no," the giant answered, shaking his massive head. "No one comes to me. I am Night-Walker. All who see and hear me are afraid."

Then Dawn-Strider laughed, and each sound was a spark of light in the dark. "I am not afraid."

But the giant did not understand. For seven days and seven nights he kept the stone rolled across the entrance to his cave. And for seven days and seven nights no sun shone upon the earth. For without Dawn-Strider to lead the way, the sun did not know which road to follow and so stayed hidden beyond the rim of the world.

Outside the cave it was as dark as within. Up the mountains and down, through hill towns and valleys, in low places and high, darkness reigned. And the world was dimly lit by the moon and flickering stars.

Plants withered and began to die. Trees shed their leaves. The little animals huddled in their burrows. And by their dying hearthfires the people shivered, waiting for the sun.

Only Night-Walker was happy in his cave, listening to Dawn-Strider's light-filled laughter and watching the bright child dressed in red and gold.

Finally, after seven days as dark as seven nights, the people bundled themselves into their clothes. They met in the court-yards and doorways of the towns or talked in the meadows.

Some said it was a curse. Others said it was the end of the world. But then someone said, "It is the giant. It is Night-Walker. *He* has stolen the sun." And everyone agreed.

But they could not agree how they could make the giant return the sun. None of them dared face him. They believed that to look upon his face or to hear his voice would turn them to stone.

After many cold meetings, the people decided to choose someone by lot. The chosen one would go up to the giant's cave and beg for the return of the sun. Then he would run back as fast as he could. If he were lucky, he would not have to see or hear Night-Walker at all.

The lots were drawn, and the short stick fell to a small child. His mother wept and his father cursed, but neither was allowed to take the child's place. "After all, it was fairly chosen," said the villagers. So the child had to go, alone, up to the giant's cave.

Behind him, safely hidden by bushes and trees, yet close enough so they could watch the child's progress, were all the people.

With his head down and feet scuffling the ground be-fore him, the child trudged up the hill toward the cave. When he stood at last before the stone door, the child called out in a tiny voice, "Night-Walker, giant, return our sun."

For a few moments nothing happened. The child sighed, and started to turn back down the hill. But suddenly a grumbling was heard from the cave's entrance, and the stone started to roll aside.

Shaking his shaggy hair in the light of the moon, Night-Walker stepped out. He glared at the miserable child. The child was so frightened, he could not move. He stood like stone. And the people who had come to watch ran screaming and stumbling back to their homes.

The giant looked down and picked up the child in his hand. "What do you mean by disturbing me? Don't you know I am Night-Walker? I am the Watcher in the Gloom?"

The child was amazed that he could still blink and twitch after gazing on Night-Walker's face and hearing his voice. He managed to cry out, "Our . . . our sun. Give us back our sun."

"Bah! I do not have your sun," said Night-Walker.

"But you have me," said a small voice by the giant's side. "And with me comes the sun." It was Dawn-Strider, stepping out of the cave.

The child from the lottery looked down over the giant's cupped hand. And when he saw another child moving and laughing by the giant's side, he was no longer afraid. He smiled at Dawn-Strider. He even smiled at the giant.

Night-Walker was so surprised that, without thinking, he

21

smiled back. And as he smiled, the sun so long hidden from the world rose up over the mountains.

The people who had been hastily stumbling back to their homes were stopped by the unexpected dawn. "The giant has given us back our sun," they called joyously to one another, and they turned back to the cave.

When they got to the top of the hill, they found the giant still standing there. He was smiling, with a child in each hand. The three new friends were laughing and talking —even singing in their joy.

Now that he had friends who did not find him fearsome to look upon, the giant gave up walking at night. He lived for the coming of the sun each day. And Dawn-Strider always visited the giant's cave-castle home first, bringing the sun there before anywhere else in the whole world.

The giant gave rides to all the children of the village in his outstretched palms every morning of the year. And he was known as Sun-Walker ever after.

THE WEAVER
OF TOMORROW

Once, on the far side of yesterday, there lived a girl who wanted to know the future. She was not satisfied with knowing that the grass would come up each spring and that the sun would go down each night. The true knowledge she desired was each tick of tomorrow, each fall and each failure, each heartache and each pain, that would be the portion of every man. And because of this wish of hers, she was known as Vera, which is to say *True*.

At first it was easy enough. She lived simply in a simple town, where little happened to change a day but a birth or a death that was always expected. And Vera awaited each event at the appointed bedside and, in this way, was always the first to know.

But as with many wishes of the heart, hers grew from a wish to a desire, from a desire to an obsession. And soon, knowing the simple futures of the simple people in that simple town was not enough for her.

"I wish to know what tomorrow holds for everyone," said Vera. "For every man and woman in our country. For every man and woman in our world."

"It is not good, this thing you wish," said her father.

But Vera did not listen. Instead she said, "I wish to know

which king will fall and what the battle, which queen will die and what the cause. I want to know how many mothers will cry for babies lost and how many wives will weep for husbands slain."

And when she heard this, Vera's mother made the sign against the Evil One, for it was said in their simple town that the future was the Devil's dream.

But Vera only laughed and said loudly, "And for that, I want to know what the Evil One himself is doing with *his* tomorrow."

Since the Evil One himself could not have missed her speech, the people of the town visited the Mayor and asked him to send Vera away.

The Mayor took Vera and her mother and father, and they sought out the old man who lived in the mountain who would answer one question a year. And they asked him what to do about Vera.

The old man who lived in the mountain, who ate the seeds that flowers dropped and the berries that God wrought, and who knew all about yesterdays and cared little about tomorrow, said, "She must be apprenticed to the Weaver."

"A weaver!" said the Mayor and Vera's father and her mother all at once. They thought surely that the old man who lived in the mountain had at last gone mad.

But the old man shook his head. "Not *a* weaver, but *the* Weaver, the Weaver of Tomorrow. She weaves with a golden

thread and finishes each piece with a needle so fine that each minute of the unfolding day is woven into her work. They say that once every hundred years there is need for an apprentice, and it is just that many years since one has been found."

"Where does one find this Weaver?" asked the Mayor.

"Ah, that I cannot say," said the old man who lived in the mountain, "for I have answered one question already." And he went back to his cave and rolled a stone across the entrance, a stone small enough to let the animals in but large enough to keep the townspeople out.

"Never mind," said Vera. "I would be apprenticed to this Weaver. And not even the Devil himself can keep me from finding her."

And so saying, she left the simple town with nothing but the clothes upon her back. She wandered until the hills got no higher but the valleys got deeper. She searched from one cold moon until the next. And at last, without warning, she came upon a cave where an old woman in black stood waiting.

"You took the Devil's own time coming," said the old woman.

"It was not his time at all," declared Vera.

"Oh, but it was," said the old woman, as she led the girl into the cave.

And what a wondrous place the cave was. On one wall hung

27

skeins of yarn of rainbow colors. On the other walls were tapestries of delicate design. In the center of the cave where a single shaft of sunlight fell was the loom of polished ebony, higher than a man and three times as broad, with a shuttle that flew like a captive black bird through the golden threads of the warp.

For a year and a day, Vera stayed in the cave apprenticed to the Weaver. She learned which threads wove the future of kings and princes and which of peasants and slaves. She was first to know in which kingdoms the sun would set and which kingdoms would be gone before the sun rose again. And though she was not yet allowed to weave, she watched the black loom where each minute of the day took shape, and learned how, once it had been woven, no power could change its course. Not an emperor, not a slave, not the Weaver herself. And she was taught to finish the work with a golden thread and a needle so fine that no one could tell where one day ended and the next began. And for a year she was happy.

But finally the day dawned when Vera was to start her second year with the Weaver. It began as usual. Vera rose and set the fire. Then she removed the tapestry of yesterday from the loom and brushed it outside until the golden threads mirrored the morning sun. She hung it on a silver hook that was by the entrance to the cave. Finally she returned to the loom which waited mutely for the golden warp to be strung.

And each thread that Vera pulled tight sang like the string of a harp. When she was through, Vera set the pot on the fire and woke the old woman to begin the weaving.

The old woman creaked and muttered as she stretched herself up. But Vera paid her no heed. Instead, she went to the Wall of Skeins and picked at random the colors to be woven. And each thread was a life.

"Slowly, slowly," the old Weaver had cautioned when Vera first learned to choose the threads. "At the end of each thread is the end of a heartbeat; the last of each color is the last of a world." But Vera could not learn to choose slowly, carefully. Instead she plucked and picked like a gay bird in the seed.

"And so it was with me," said the old Weaver with a sigh. "And so it was at first with me."

Now a year had passed, and the old woman kept her counsel to herself as Vera's fingers danced through the threads. Now she went creaking and muttering to the loom and began to weave. And now Vera turned her back to the growing cloth that told the future and took the pot from the fire to make their meal. But as soon as that was done, she would hurry back to watch the growing work, for she never wearied of watching the minutes take shape on the ebony loom.

Only this day, as her back was turned, the old woman uttered a cry. It was like a sudden sharp pain. And the silence after it was like the release from pain altogether.

29

Vera was so startled she dropped the pot, and it spilled over and sizzled the fire out. She ran to the old woman who sat staring at the growing work. There, in the gold and shimmering tapestry, the Weaver had woven her own coming death.

There was the cave and there the dropped pot; and last the bed where, with the sun shining full on her face, the old woman would breathe no more.

"It has come," the old woman said to Vera, smoothing her black skirts over her knees. "The loom is yours." She stood up fresher and younger than Vera had ever seen her, and moved with a springy joy to the bed. Then she straightened the covers and lay down, her face turned toward the entrance of the cave. A shaft of light fell on her feet and began to move, as the sun moved, slowly towards her head.

"No," cried Vera at the smiling woman. "I want the loom. But not this way."

Gently, with folded hands, the old Weaver said, "Dear child, there is no other way."

"Then," said Vera slowly, knowing she lied, but lying nonetheless, "I do not want it."

"The time for choosing is past," said the old Weaver. "You chose and your hands have been chosen. It is woven. It is so."

"And in a hundred years?" asked Vera.

"You will be the Weaver, and some young girl will come, bright and eager, and you will know your time is near."

32

"No," said Vera.

"It is birth," said the old Weaver.

"No," said Vera.

"It is death," said the old Weaver.

A single golden thread snapped suddenly on the loom.

Then the sun moved onto the Weaver's face and she died.

Vera sat staring at the old woman but did not stir. And though she sat for hour upon hour, and the day grew cold, the sun did not go down. Battles raged on and on, but no one won and no one lost for nothing more had been woven.

At last, shivering with the cold, though the sun was still high, Vera went to the loom. She saw the old woman buried and herself at work, and so she hastened to the tasks.

And when the old woman lay under an unmarked stone in a forest full of unmarked stones, with only Vera to weep her down, Vera returned to the cave.

Inside, the loom gleamed black, like a giant ebony cage with golden bars as thin and fine as thread. And as Vera sat down to finish the weaving, her bones felt old and she welcomed the shaft of sun as it crept across her back. She welcomed each trip of the shuttle through the warp as it ticked off the hundred years to come. And at last Vera knew all she wanted to know about the future.

THE LAD WHO
STARED
EVERYONE DOWN

Once there was a lad who was so proud, he was determined to stare everyone in the world down.

He began in the farmyard of his father's house. He stared into the eyes of the chickens until the cock's feathers drooped and the hens ran cackling from his gaze.

"What a fine eye," thought the lad "They are all afraid of me." And he went to stare down the cows.

The cows turned their velvety eyes to watch the boy approach. He never turned his head but stared and stared until the herd turned away in confusion and clattered down to the meadow gate.

"They are all afraid. See them run," thought the lad. And he went to stare down his mother and father.

At the table he glared at his parents until his father dropped his knife and his mother started to weep.

"Why are you doing this?" they cried. "No good can come of such staring."

But the lad never said a word. He packed his handkerchief with a few provisions—a loaf of brown bread, some cheese, and a flask of ginger beer—and went out to stare down the world.

He walked a day and a night and came at last to the walls of a great town.

"Let me in," he called out to the old watchman, "for I have stared down fathers and mothers, I have stared down a host of herdsmen. I have stared down strangers in a farmyard, and I can stare you down, too."

The watchman trembled when he heard this, but he did not let the lad come in. "Stare away," he said in a wavery voice.

The lad came nearer to the watchman and stared into the old man's watery eyes. He stared steadily till the old man felt weak with hunger and faint with standing, and at last the old man glanced away.

Without another word, the lad marched in through the gate and on into the town.

He walked until he came to the door of the castle where two handsome soldiers in their bright red coats stood at attention and gazed into space.

The lad looked at them and thought, "I have stared down a mighty watchman, I have stared down fathers and mothers, I have stared down a host of herdsmen, I have stared down strangers in a farmyard, and I can stare down these two."

The soldiers glanced the lad's way. The lad stared back. He stared and stared until a passing fly caused one of the soldiers to sneeze.

"That mere lad has stared you down," whispered the other soldier to his companion, out of the side of his mouth.

"No, he didn't," said the one who had looked away.

"Yes, he did!" said the other.

And soon they fell to fighting.

While they were squabbling and quarreling, the lad slipped in through the door and marched till he came to a great hall. There was the king, sitting on his throne.

The lad marched right up to the king who was sitting silent in all his majesty. He stared at the king and the king stared back.

As the lad stared, he thought, "I have stared down quarrelsome soldiers, I have stared down a mighty watchman, I have stared down fathers, I have stared down mothers, I have stared down a host of herdsmen, I have stared down strangers in the farmyard, and I can stare you down, too."

As the lad stared, the king thought, "What a strange, mad lad. He must be taken away." And he turned to speak to his councilor about the staring lad.

"See, see," thought the lad, "I have stared down the king himself. They are all afraid of me."

And without a word, he marched out the door and into the courtyard, through the courtyard and out into the town square.

"Hear ye, hear ye," he shouted to the crowd that quickly gathered. "I am the lad who stared everyone down. I have stared down the king of kings, I have stared down quarrelsome soldiers, I have stared down a mighty watchman, I have stared down fathers, I have stared down mothers, I have stared down a host of herdsmen, I have stared down strangers in the farm-yard. I have stared everyone down. There is no one greater than I."

The crowd oohed and the crowd aahed, and the crowd made a thousand obeisances. Except for one old man who had seen everything and believed nothing.

"No good will come of all this staring," said the old man.

The lad merely stared at the old man and laughed. "And I can stare you down, too," he said.

"I am sure you can," said the old man. "But staring down an old man is no problem at all for a lad who has stared *everyone* down."

The lad looked uneasy for the first time.

Then the old man pointed to the sun that glowered like a red eye in the sky. "But if you can stare that down," he said, "I will believe your boast."

"Done," said the proud lad, and he turned his face to the sky.

All that day the lad stared at the sun. And as he stared, the sun seemed to grow and change and blossom. He stared until the sun had burned its image into his eyes.

And when at last night came, the sun went down. Yet still the boy kept staring.

The crowd shouted, "He has done it. He has done it. He has stared the sun down, too."

Even the old man nodded his head at the marvel and turned to shake the lad's hand.

But the proud lad thrust the hand aside. "Quiet, you fools.

Quiet. Can't you see the sun? It is shining still. It shines on and on. Quiet, for I must keep on staring until I have stared it down. I am the lad who stares everyone down."

The sun came up again and the sun went down again, but the boy never moved. And as far as anyone knows, the proud lad is staring still.

SILENT BIANCA

Once far to the North, where the world is lighted only by the softly flickering snow, a strange and beautiful child was born.

Her face was like crystal with the features etched in. And she was called Bianca, a name that means "white," for her face was pale as snow and her hair was white as a moonbeam.

As Bianca grew to be a young woman, she never spoke as others speak. Instead her words were formed soundlessly into tiny slivers of ice. And if a person wanted to know what she was saying, he had to pluck her sentences out of the air before they fell to the ground or were blown away by the chilling wind. Then each separate word had to be warmed by the hearthfire until at last the room was filled with the delicate sounds of Bianca's voice. They were strange sounds and as fragile as glass.

At first many people came to see the maiden and to catch her words. For it was said that she was not only beautiful but wise as well.

But the paths to her hut were few. For the frost cut cruelly at every step. And it took so long to talk with Bianca that after a while, no one came to visit her at all.

Now it happened that the king of the vast country where Bianca lived was seeking a wife who was both beautiful and wise. But when he asked his council how to find such a bride, the councilors scratched their heads and stroked their beards and managed to look full of questions and answers at the same time.

"Can you do such a thing?" asked one. "Can you not do such a thing?" asked another. "How is it possible?" asked a third. And they spent a full day looking up to the ceiling and down to the floor and answering each question with another.

At last the king said, "Enough of this useless noise. I will find a way and I will find a woman. And the one who will be my bride will be filled with silence and still speak more wisdom than any of you."

At that the councilors left off talking and began to laugh. For it was well known that wisdom was to be found in things said, not in silence. And it was also known that no one—not even the king—was as wise as the members of the king's council.

But the king sent his most trusted servant, a gentle old painter named Piers, to the corners of the kingdom. Piers was to talk with all the maidens of noble birth. Then he was to bring back portraits of the most beautiful of these from which the king might choose a bride.

Piers traveled many days and weeks. He wearied himself in the great halls and draughty palaces listening to the chattering, nattering maidens who wanted to marry the king. At last, his saddlebags filled with their portraits and his mind packed with their prattle, he started for home.

On his way home from the cold lands, Piers became lost

in a fierce snowstorm. He was forced to seek shelter in a nearby hut. It was the hut where Bianca made her home. Piers meant to stay but a single day. But one day whitened into a second and then a third. It was soon a week that the old man had remained there, talking to Bianca and warming her few words by the fire. He never told her who he was or what his mission. If she guessed, she never said. Indeed, in *not* saying lay much of her wisdom.

At last the storm subsided and Piers returned to the king's castle. In his saddlebags he carried large portraits of the most beautiful noble maidens in the kingdom. But the old man carried on a chain around his neck a miniature portrait of Bianca. She had become like a daughter to him. The thought of her was like a calm, cool breeze in the warmer lands where he lived.

When the day came for the king to make his choice, all of the king's council assembled in the Great Hall. Piers drew the large portraits from his saddlebags one by one and recalled what the maidens had spoken. The king and his council looked at the pictures and heard the words. And one by one they shook their heads.

As Piers bent to put the final portrait back into his pack, the chain with the miniature slipped out of his doublet. The king reached over and touched it. Then he held it up to the light and looked at the picture.

"Who is this?" he asked. "And why is this portrait smaller and set apart from the rest?"

Piers answered, "It is a maiden known as Bianca. She lives in the cold lands far to the North. She speaks in slivers that cut through lies." And he told them about the storm and how he had met the beautiful, silent girl and discovered her great wisdom.

"This is the one I shall marry," said the king.

"It would be most improper," said the councilors together. "She is not noble-born."

"How does one judge nobility?" asked the king. "How does one measure it?"

The councilors scratched their heads and looked puzzled. "Can you do such a thing?" asked one. "Can you not do such a thing?" said another. "How is it possible?" asked a third. And they continued this way for some time.

At last the king silenced them with his hand. "Enough of this noise. I will make a measure. I will test the wisdom of this Silent Bianca," he said. And under his breath, he added, "And I will test *your* wisdom as well."

Then the king sent his council, with Piers to guide them, off to the cold lands to bring Bianca back to the throne.

Piers and the councilors traveled twenty days and nights until the stars fell like snow behind them and at last they came to the chilly land where Bianca made her home. There they packed up Bianca and her few belongings and immediately started back to the king.

But when they reached the road that ran around the castle, strange to say, they found their way blocked by soldiers.

Campfires blossomed like flowers on the plain. At every turning and every straightaway stood a guard. It seemed there was no place where they could pass.

"This is very odd," said Piers. "There have never been soldiers here before. Could some unknown enemy have captured the castle while we were away?"

The councilors tried to question the guards, but none would answer. Not even a single question. Unused to silence, the councilors fell to puzzling among themselves. Some said one thing and some said another. They talked until the sun burned out behind them, but they could figure out no way to get beyond the guards and so bring Bianca to the king.

The air grew cold. The dark drew close. The councilors, weary with wondering, slept.

Only Bianca, who had said nothing all this time, remained awake. When she was certain that all the councilors were asleep, and even Piers was snoring gently, Bianca arose. Slowly she walked along the road that circled around the castle. Now and then she opened her mouth as if to scream or speak or sigh. But of course no sounds came out of her mouth at all. Then she would close it again, kneeling humbly when challenged by a silent guard's upraised spear. For the guards still spoke not a word but remained closemouthed at their posts.

And so from path to path, from guard to guard, from campfire to campfire, Bianca walked.

Just at dawn, she returned to the place where the councilors and Piers slept leaning on one another's shoulders like sticks stacked up ready for a fire.

As the sun flamed into the sky, a sudden strange babble was heard. At first it was like a single woman crying, calling, sobbing. Then, as the sun grew hotter and the morning cook-fires were lit, it was as though a thousand women called to their men, wailing and sighing at each campfire and at every turning. It was the slivers of Bianca's voice which she had so carefully placed during her long night's walk; the slivers warmed and melted by the rising sun and the burning coals.

But the guards did not know this. And they looked around one way and another. Yet the only woman near them was Bianca, sitting silently, smiling, surrounded by Piers and the puzzled councilors.

And then, from somewhere beyond the guards, a chorus of women cried out. It was a cry like a single clear voice. "Come home, come home," called the women. "Leave off your soldiering. You need no arms but ours. Leave off your soldiering. No arms . . . no arms but ours."

The guards hesitantly at first, by ones and twos, and then joyfully by twenties and hundreds, threw down their weapons. Then they raced back home to their wives and sweethearts. For they were not really an unknown enemy at all but towns-men hired by the king to try the wisdom of the councilors and of Bianca.

When the councilors realized what Bianca had done, they brought her swiftly to the king. Instead of scratching their heads and looking puzzled, they spoke right out and said, "She is most certainly wise and more than fit for a king to marry."

The king, when he heard how Bianca had fooled the guards, laughed and laughed for he thought it a grand joke. And when he stopped laughing and considered the meaning of her words, he agreed she was indeed even wiser than old Piers had said.

So the king and Bianca were married.

And if the king had any problems thereafter, and his council could give him only questions instead of answers, he might be found at the royal hearthstone. There he could be seen warming his hands. But he was doing something more besides: He would be listening to the words that came from the fire and from the wise and loving heart of Silent Bianca, his queen.

ABOUT THE AUTHOR

Jane Yolen is known especially for her rare ability to create modern stories in the vein of the great classic folktales. Her poetic prose has won her many awards and honors. Born in New York, she is a graduate of Smith College. She worked for a time as an editor of children's books before she decided to become a full-time writer. She is married and lives with her husband and their three small children in a lovely old house in Hatfield, Massachusetts. Among her many distinguished books are *The Wizard Islands, The Bird of Time*, and *The Girl Who Loved the Wind*.

ABOUT THE ILLUSTRATOR

David Palladini was born in Italy, but came to the United States when he was very young and grew up in Highland Park, Illinois. He received his art training at Pratt Institute in Brooklyn, New York. In addition to illustrating books, Mr. Palladini has received many awards and citations for his work in poster design and the graphic arts.

Library of Congress Cataloging in Publication Data

Yolen, Jane.
  The girl who cried flowers and other tales.

  Reprint of the ed. published by Crowell, New York.
  CONTENTS: The girl who cried flowers.—Dawn-strider.
—The weaver of tomorrow.—The lad who stared everyone
down.—[etc.]
  1. Fairy tales, American. 2. Children's stories,
American. [1. Fairy tales. 2. Short stories]
I. Palladini, David. II. Title.
[PZ8.Y78Gf   1981   [Fic]   80-26140